P9-DDB-246

Gg Hh Ii Jj Kk Ll Mm

Uu Vv Ww Xx Yy Zz

Dear Parent,

The My First Steps to Reading® *series is based on a teaching activity that helps children learn to recognize letters and their sounds. The use of predictable language patterns and repetition of familiar words will also help your child build a basic sight vocabulary. Your child will enjoy watching the characters in the books place imaginative objects in "letter boxes." You and your child can even create and fill your own letter box, using stuffed animals, cut-out pictures, or other objects beginning with the same letter. The things you can do together are limited only by your imagination. Learning letters will be fun—the first important step on the road to reading.*

The Editors

© 2001 The Child's World, Inc.
All Rights Reserved. Published by Scholastic Inc., 90 Old Sherman Turnpike, Danbury, Connecticut 06810,
by arrangement with The Child's World, Inc.
Scholastic offers a varied selection of children's book racks and tote bags. For details about ordering, please write to:
Scholastic At Home, 90 Old Sherman Turnpike, Danbury, CT 06810, Attention: Premium Department

Originally published as *My "i" Sound Box* by The Child's World, Inc.

My First Steps to Reading is a registered trademark of Grolier Publishing Co. Inc.
SCHOLASTIC and associated logos are trademarks and/or registered trademarks of Scholastic Inc.

No part of this publication may be reproduced, or stored in a retrieval system, or transmitted in any form or by any means,
electronic, mechanical, photocopying, recording, or otherwise, without written permission of the publisher.
For information regarding permission, write to The Child's World, Inc., P.O. Box 326, Chanhassen, MN 55317.
ISBN 0-7172-6508-0

Printed in the U.S.A.

My "i" Book

(This book concentrates on the short "i" sound in the story line.
Words beginning with the long "i" sound are
included at the end of the book.)

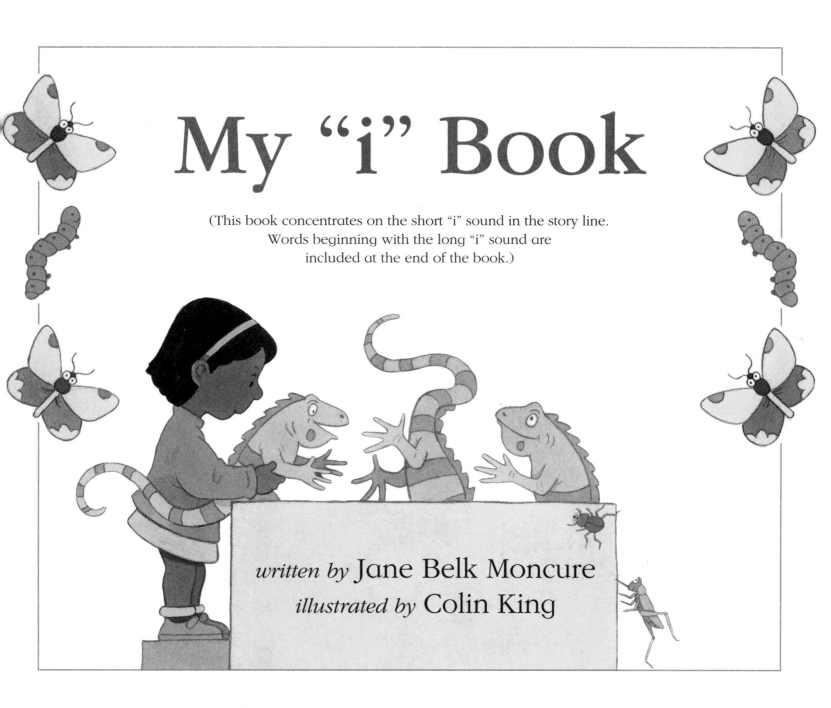

written by Jane Belk Moncure
illustrated by Colin King

Little  had a box.

"I will find things that begin
with my 'i' sound," she said.

"I will put them into
my sound box."

Little went skip, skip, skip up a hill.

She found inchworms,

lots of inchworms.

The inchworms wiggled and wiggled.

"What wiggly inchworms," she said.

Did she put the inchworms
into her box? She did.

Then Little  found iguanas,

lots of iguanas.

The iguanas wiggled and wiggled.

"What wiggly iguanas," she said.

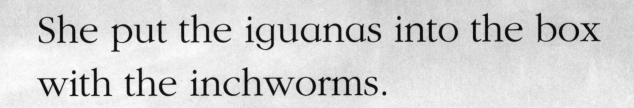

She put the iguanas into the box
with the inchworms.

But the inchworms did not like
the iguanas!

The inchworms jumped out of the box.

The iguanas jumped, too.

Away they went!

Little i could not find

the inchworms or . . .

the iguanas.

They were hiding.

Then Little i found an igloo.

Did she put the igloo into her box?
She did.

Just then, the sun came out.
Guess what?

The igloo melted.

"Now who will help me
fill my box?" she asked.

A friend came by.

"I will help you," he said.

"We can fill your box with insects."

First they found big green insects,

lots of big green insects.

Next, they found yellow insects
and brown insects.

Then they found red and black insects.
"What else can we do?" asked Little .

"We can make an insect zoo," said her friend.

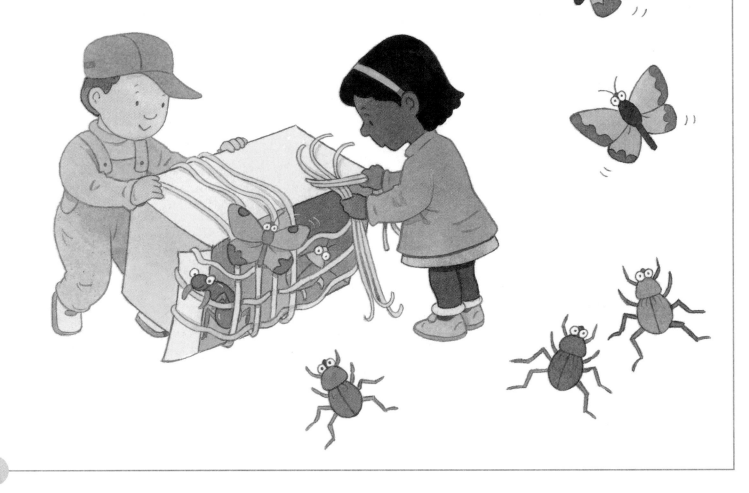

"We'll have all kinds of insects!"

Can you read these words

with Little  ?

ink

inn

invitation

instruments

Little  has another sound in some words. She says her name, "i."

Can you read these words? Listen for Little's name.

ice skates

island

ice cubes

ice cream

Aa Bb Cc Dd Ee Ff

Nn Oo Pp Qq Rr Ss Tt

My First
Steps to
READING®